For Claudia and Jack — who taught me to fly
G. R.

For my friends Pat, Cheryl, Mia, and Tom —
who taught me how to land
M. M.

A note to parents and caregivers:

Explain to your kids
that no one can fly
with only a sheet —
make sure they don't try.

Text copyright © 2012 by Gary Ross
Illustrations copyright © 2012 by Matthew Myers

First edition 2012

Library of Congress Cataloging-in-Publication Data is available.
Library of Congress Catalog Card Number pending
ISBN 978-0-7636-4920-3

12 13 14 15 16 17 LEO 10 9 8 7 6 5 4 3 2 1
Printed in Heshan, Guangdong, China

This book was typeset in Chaparral.
Title calligraphy by Judythe Sieck
The illustrations were done in oil.

Candlewick Press
99 Dover Street
Somerville, Massachusetts 02144

visit us at www.candlewick.com

BARTHOLOMEW BIDDLE
and the Very Big Wind

by GARY ROSS

illustrated by MATTHEW MYERS

CANDLEWICK PRESS

It was a cold, bitter wind,
and it blew . . . and it blew. . . .
It blew through the trees
and the little town, too.

It blew past the houses
where children were sleeping.
It blew through the keyholes
where peepers were peeping.

It blew down the streets
that were shrouded in slumber.
It rattled the rooftops
right down to the lumber.

It whistled past lampposts,
screamed over the lake,
all in search of a boy
who was still wide awake. . . .

Now, Bartholomew stood
at the window and stared.
He wasn't much drowsy
and wasn't much scared.

All that commotion
was pretty exciting —
a celestial battle
the heavens were fighting!

"Why, that looks like fun!
Just look at those trees!
They're bending in half —
yeah, that's quite a breeze."

Bart thought for a moment
and glanced toward his bed.
He could hide in the covers
or maybe instead

grab the sheet and his nerve,
seize the moment at hand.
He stretched the sheet wide
and came up with a plan:

why, this silly old wind
was nothing to fear
with a bedsheet to sail
and an instinct to steer.

He could ride through the storm
right into the night,
take off like a rocket —
a Bartholomew kite!

He reached for the window
and summoned his strength,
stood up on his toes
to his full five-foot length . . .

Bartholomew gave it
a pull, then a push,
and then *alacazam*!
In one great big *whoosh*

his toys hit the ceiling,
his books hit the floor,
his homework went reeling
right out the door!

This wasn't a breeze —
it was safe to assume
the *Grandaddy of Winds*
had blown straight to his room!

So Bartholomew grabbed
either end of his sheet.
He steadied his grip
and looked down toward the street.

He stood on the sill,
put his arms to his sides,
and that's how Bartholomew
took quite a ride.

"Oh, my gosh! Oh, my God!
I mean — this is *insane*!"
(He'd turned from a ten-year-old
to a small plane.)

The houses all looked
like the toys in his room.
If genies had carpets,
and witches had brooms,

then what was he doing
up here with a *sheet*?
He banked to his left
and looked down at the street.

The cars seemed so small
you could move 'em around
like your own little world.
He thought, *Hmm . . . Biddletown.*

Biddleberg? Biddleland?
Biddleworld? He'd be *king.*
Emperor Biddle . . .
it had a nice ring.

Bartholomew tilted
a bit to his right —
the sheet cornered nicely,
just like a new bike.

He tugged on the corners
and soared through the sky.
He pulled in the edges
and started to *fly.*

"Wow, this isn't bad!"
he said, swooping and soaring,
buzzing the rooftops while
people were snoring.

"If I took this to school,
I'd make pretty good time."
Then he pointed straight up
and started to climb.

Bartholomew laughed
as the bedsheet rose higher.
He imagined himself
"The World's Best Bedsheet Flier."

"I'm sure that there's someone
in France or Brazil
who can fly one of these things
as well as I will

"once I practice a while,
but right now I'm *it,*
at least here in Fairview."
And right then he got hit

with a pretty huge gust
that shot him up higher,
testing the skill
of the Best Bedsheet Flier.

Bart pulled on the ends,
and smoothed out the sail.
He leveled 'er off —
he had no plans to bail.

He liked this new life,
living lighter than air.
"Hmmm — this isn't bad. . . .
Now, let's go somewhere."

Arrrgh, aye.
And a billagumrump.
Scalalway creekish on me
crickasahw stump.

Well, that's a strange language,"
Bartholomew said.
He'd spent the whole night
in a strange treetop bed.

From his perch in a palm frond
he looked at the beach.
Above him, bananas
hung just out of reach.

I'm hungry, he thought,
and it's cereal time.
At home, Mom'd be yelling
like his life was a crime:

"Young man, you are now
over nine minutes late.
It's ten to the bus stop,
and buses don't wait.

"So go brush your teeth,
and then feed the cat,
and remember your sweater,
and *please* not that hat.

"It's torn, and it's tattered
and covered with gunk.
You'll look like an urchin
and smell like a skunk!"

And right about then
it would all turn to noise.
He'd head for the bus stop
like dozens of boys

with noise in their heads
and their moms in their ears,
but up in this tree
there was something to *hear*:

Scour an' swabby
a fifewhistle blowin,
saltair n shanties
t' keep the lads rowin'.

To say they were pirates
was putting it mildly.
They were waving their arms
and doing so wildly,

with pegs on their legs
and gold in their ears
and spiral tattoos —
a sight to be feared.

They were snarling and sneering
and laughing and grinning.
One had a parrot,
and that's just the beginning.

One had a bright crimson
patch on his eyeball;
one had a cutlass
for cutting down rivals.

One's name was Smee
and one Mr. Jynx;
one had a ring in the shape
of the sphinx.

One brandished pistols;
another had daggers.
They looked up at Bart
with a pirate-like swagger.

They sneered and they leered,
looking up at his tree.
*I bet their next victim
is going to be me!*

But then he remembered,
*It's cereal time.
A bunch of bananas
might do them just fine.*

*If it's booty they're after,
well, what could be better
than nice ripe bananas
and a good fuzzy sweater?*

Bart reached above him
and managed to grab 'em.
He forced a big smile, saying,
"Here, you can have 'em.

"And also my sweater —
it's genuine cashmere.
Take all that I've got —
now, what else do I have here?"

He tossed all the fruit
to the big guy in charge,
a man ten feet tall
and wide as a barge,

who glanced at the tree
with a sneer that seemed spiteful,
then took the bananas,
saying, "My, how delightful!

"It seems our young friend here
has graced us with fruit.
He's given us breakfast
and clothing to boot.

"What a charming young fellow!
Why, we should be gracious.
You can have my own hammock —
it's so much more spacious

"than this *tree* you've selected.
Though I like the location,
there's much nicer ways
to spend your vacation!

"Tonight we'll prepare you
a wonderful feast.
It's the least we can do —
you've flown in from the east!"

"But you all seem so *nice,*"
Bartholomew said.
(And they *were* looking nicer
now that they'd been fed.)

"Well, of course we do,"
said the man with a laugh.
"Even pirates have manners.
You'd have to be daft

"to go through this life
judging books by their covers.
If you jump to conclusions,
what's left to discover?

"So, you thought we were all
just some nasty marauders,
larcenous thieves,
and petty defrauders?

"But nothing, you see,
could be further from true.
I mean, why do we *all*
do the things that we do?

"The rings in our noses,
the parrots, the rum —
we just do that stuff
because it is *fun!*"

For the next several weeks
Bart lived in a dream —
no homework, no bedtime,
no little league team.

That stuff wasn't bad
but kids need a break.
He ate coconut crumpets
and pineapple cake,

with a boatload of pirates
whose ship was abandoned —
well, more like "ignored"
since they all hit the land in

this magical place
where the Trade Windies blew.
No, they wouldn't trade it
and neither would you!

Bart swam in the ocean
and slept in the sand.
He gave rides on the bedsheet
for five hundred grand.

"Oh, just pay me later,"
he'd say with a smile.
"If we get to ten million,
we'll stop for a while."

In the evenings they'd
listen to tropical tunes
banged out on marimbas
with fine silver spoons.

The captain explained,
"What good is a treasure
all locked in a chest?
And then for good measure

"you bury the stuff
and then you never use it
and then make a map
so that you never lose it.

"I'd much rather have it
right here on the beach,
to touch it and spend it
and keep it in reach."

They danced by the fire;
they climbed in the trees.
For almost four weeks
they did as they pleased.

Then one day when he
was out gathering sea glass,
Bartholomew heard something
sniff as he passed.

He stopped and went back,
as the sniffles got louder.
They snorted and snuffled
from inside the flowers.

It seemed for a second
a garden was crying,
but under the petals
the captain was lying.

He covered his head
and buried his face,
but still there were tears
all over the place.

"What's wrong?" asked Bartholomew,
leaning in closer.
The man shook his head
and shruggled his shoulders.

"I don't know," he said.
"We have nothing but fun,
but after a while
the doing is done,

"and the gladder you try,
the sadder you get,
and you gladden some more,
but you're stuck in this net,

"because fun isn't fun
when it's all that you know.
It may look like fun,
but it's just a big show."

He heaved a big sigh
and stared at the ground.
Bartholomew nodded
then looked all around.

The island was perfect,
like heaven times ten!
But you know, even heaven
gets old now and then

'cause tough as it was
to admit to himself,
he missed his old room
and the toys on his shelf,

and even his mom
at a quarter to eight:
"C'mon, sleepyhead —
you're one hour late!"

Yes, sometimes a kid
needs a boring-er day,
with homework and dishes. . . .
"I'd sure love to stay,

"but I gotta be going —
I mean, you know, get *flying*."
The captain fought tears
or at least he was *trying*.

"If you stay here," he nodded,
"you'll just end up like us.
You belong back at home."
And he fiddled and fussed

with a small leather pouch
that he hung from his neck.
"Here, this is for you —
a doubloon from the wreck

of the *Annie O' Grady*,
which sunk off the cape.
Remember us, will you?
You've been quite a mate."

They threw him a banquet
to say their good-byes,
with passion-fruit cupcakes
and fresh mango pies.

They gorged on bananas
with sugary frosting.
They spared no expense,
no matter the costing.

And then the next day
they all stood on the beach,
and Bartholomew took out and
unfurled his sheet.

The men bit their lips
as they looked toward the sea
(for pirates are quite
sentimental, you see.)

Bart ruffled the sheet
and felt for a breeze.
"Our good friend is leaving.
A cheer, if you please."

"Hip hip hooray!
Hip hip bye-bye!"
And then in the flash
and the blink of an eye,

a breeze whistled in
like a train to the station:
the Five Forty-two
straight from Big Windy Nation.

It filled out the sheet
and it tugged on the ends.
The trees screamed and whistled,
then started to bend . . .

Bartholomew hung on as
long as he could.
He wanted to stay
but knew that he should

give that slight little hop
that would take him away.
The best of good-byes
seemed to happen that way.

"I'll miss every one of you.
Really, I will."
A beach is much different
from window or sill,

and Bartholomew shot up
like nine hundred feet,
and then just as fast,
he started to meet

some sandpipers . . . seagulls . . .
migrating geese.
The island grew small —
it was just out of reach.

"So *that's* how a memory
happens," he said.
"One minute it's here,
then the next, in your head."

Row after row
of the same little yards,
the same little fences,
the same little cars —

even the trees
grew in long rows of ten.
They stood single file,
and so did the men

who stood at the station,
their eyes toward the ground.
Bartholomew thought,
What a sad little town.

*I'd fly right on by, but
my altitude's low.*
And since bedsheets can't climb
when the wind just won't blow,

he tugged on the ends and
began his descent.
The houses got bigger
but none dif-fer-ent.

The whole place was bathed
in a gray, blueish haze.
The men filed forward,
all lost in a daze.

There was something about it
that made Bart quite sad:
these men going to work —
and he thought of his dad. . . .

Was he like that, too,
each morning at nine?
Well, eight fifty-seven
and always on time.

Where does he go
when he kisses good-bye,
when he leaves with a wave
saying, "Bye-bye — gotta fly!"?

Each morning and night
he'd pass through that door,
but what comes in the middle?
There's got to be more

for Benjamin Biddle,
VP of Accounts,
who told Bart one day,
"Be whatever you want.

"You're young, and the future
is yours to be plucked.
Of course, you'll need effort
and lots of good luck,

"but here are some crayons.
There are five hundred shades!
There's Ferndale Green
and Everest Glades.

"There's Cobalt and Basalt
and Aquamarine —
all sorts of colors
that *I've* never seen."

He spoke in a whisper
as if it was private.
His son whispered back.
Bartholomew liked it

'cause this was their secret,
right there in that box:
five hundred colors!
And neither would talk.

They just stared at that rainbow,
complete in their hands.
And as his mind wandered,
Bart's forehead went . . . *bam!*

His arm clipped a tree,
upending the craft.
Instead of an airplane,
it turned to a raft

that splashed in a pond
that was covered with muck.
There were lots of dead leaves
and a family of ducks.

Bart emerged from the pond
with gunk in his nose
and gunk in his ears
and gunk in his toes,

and right then he heard
the familiar-ist sound:
a school bell was ringing
and shaking the ground.

All school bells are loud,
but this one was worse.
It rattled your bones
like a dark school-bell curse.

Bartholomew peeked
through the leaves on the bank,
and there, in the distance . . .
His heart really sank.

The boys filed out,
looking just like the men.
They all walked precisely,
each clutching a pen.

They wore the same jackets.
They wore the same shoes.
They wore the same shirts
in the same shades of blues.

But Bartholomew thought
he must look even odder
with slime on his head,
all drenched in pond water.

You flew here alone?”
the loudest one said.
“Without supervision?
Or a note signed in red?”

“I just kind of landed,”
Bartholomew answered.
“No Rudolph, no sleigh,
no Prancer, no Dancer.

“In fact I just blew here
with only a sheet.”
And this made them murmur
and glance at their feet.

“But that’s not allowed,”
the tallest one said.
“You can’t make an airplane
with things from your *bed*.”

His voice dropped an octave;
his face filled with gloom:
“You’re not s’posed to tamper
with stuff in your room.”

“I don’t even go here,”
Bartholomew said.
“I blew in from there.”
And with that, jerked his head

toward the edge of the trees,
where a dim sun was setting:
a hint of a glint.
And if you were betting,

you'd say it was the first time
they'd looked toward that light.
And then just as quickly,
they all jumped with fright,

for the school bell was clanging
its ominous clang,
and they hurried away
as it rang and it rang.

All except one,
who paused for a beat
and looked at Bartholomew,
then at the sheet,

and then squinted off
toward that last bit of day,
straining his eyes
that particular way

that everyone does when
they see something new . . .
and then just as quickly,
he ran away, too.

Bartholomew lived
for three days by the lake.
He made a nice tent
with two shovels, a rake,

and his fine trusty bedsheet
spread out like a roof.
It could do more than fly,
and this was the proof.

He fashioned a pillow
from swamp grass and leaves.
"Why, that's a nice place,"
he said, feeling quite pleased.

At night he would listen
to crickets and frogs,
an evening concerto
that came from the logs

that were sunk in the mud.
And Bartholomew listened
while moonlight shone down
in a soft silver glisten,

and as he would lie there,
the breeze would blow by,
and the trees whispered softly,
"Can I learn to fly?"

Bartholomew opened
his eyes with a start,
'cause that's a strange thing
for a tree to impart.

But it wasn't the breeze,
for there in the quiet,
a boy's face stared back.
"If you teach me, I'll try it."

He leaned in the tent
and spoke in a whisper:
"Please don't tell my parents,
my teachers, my sister.

"Nobody knows that
I snuck out to see you
or much more than that,
that I'd much rather *be* you."

And that's when he told Bart
what happened at school:
He couldn't keep track,
they had so many rules.

No running, no jumping,
no chewing of gum.
No teasing, no sneezing,
no crying for your mum.

No singing, no bringing
of items from home.
No trips to the bathroom,
at least not alone.

"The rules are the rules.
You must never ask why.
You must follow each one.
But if I learned to *fly*!"

He looked at Bartholomew,
hungry and yearning.
What good was a school
with all rules and no learning?

"Okay, then," said Bart.
"Do heights ever scare you?
Do you dare to be daring
when no one will dare you?

"Do you have an objection
to wind in your face?
Do you ever get winded
while running in place?"

"No. Yes. No and no,"
the boy quickly responded.
(In less than five minutes
they seemed to have bonded.)

"All right, then, we'll practice
right here on the lake.
We'll use an old rowboat,
this sheet, and this rake

"till you get a good sense
of the wind — how it shifts.
Sometimes it can swirl.
Sometimes it just drifts.

"And you've got to learn
how to work with the sheet;
it's different up there
from down here on the street."

The boy seemed to beam
with a gleam in his eye,
and the dream seemed to linger:
"Why, I'm gonna *fly*!"

His full name was
Densmore Horatio Pool,
so the world called him "Densy"
or sometimes "Hey, you!"

With a name like Bartholomew,
Bart sympathized —
so tough to pronounce
that no one would try.

They had more in common
than even just that:
They each had a sister,
and she had a cat.

They both hated math,
and math hated them.
They both ate their apples
right down to the stem.

Within a few days,
that rowboat was moving.
Young Densmore could steer;
his technique was improving.

"Okay," said Bartholomew,
"you're almost ready.
Your wind sense is good.
Your steering's quite steady.

"I think that it's time
to get up in the air.
There's high pressure building—
just look at the hair

"on the back of your hand,
how it stands up like that.
Some wind's coming in,
so hold on to your hat!"

Bartholomew motioned
way off toward the west:
the tree line was showing
vague signs of unrest.

"We'll meet here tomorrow
at three forty-nine.
Just bring a light jacket,
and be here *on time*."

Densy looked nervous.
"Tomorrow's not good —
I've got lots of homework,
and I really should

do the rest of my Latin
before we shove off."
Bartholomew chuckled
and stifled a scoff.

"Where *you're* going, there's only
one language, my friend.
You don't need to learn it
or write it in pen.

"You'll know it the minute
your feet leave the ground.
You'll know north from south;
you'll know up from down."

"But that's not a language,"
young Densy replied.
"That's just navigation."
Bartholomew sighed.

"You'll find out tomorrow —
it's gonna be great.
Three forty-nine
and not one minute late."

That night by the pond,
the frogs creaked and croaked.
The thrushes sang softly;
they cooed as they spoke.

Bartholomew listened
for one final time:
the crickets chimed in
with their great cricket rhyme.

By dawn he could feel
a warm breeze was blowing.
It came from the east;
a red sun was glowing.

By noon it had grown to
a nice, steady wind.
He tested the sheet —
it was time to begin.

He looked at his watch;
it was three twenty-nine.
The school bell was ringing;
there wasn't much time.

The wind blew in stronger,
now shaking the trees . . .
but no sign of Densmore.
Bart fought with the breeze.

The bedsheet was tugging
and pulling and jerking.
He glanced right and left —
maybe Densmore was working?

"Not sure I can hold it,"
Bartholomew muttered.
The bedsheet was straining —
it flapped and it fluttered.

And just then, a face
appeared in the clearing
(the nick of time, too,
for the moment was nearing).

*"You made it! You did!
Oh, I knew that you would!"*
Densmore stepped forward,
not sure that he should.

"Hurry and grab that,"
Bartholomew said.
"We've got, like, two minutes
till this blows to shreds.

"We'll balance the weight,
each one on an end."
He clung to the tree —
it started to bend.

Densmore reached out,
but his hand seemed to halt
like something had grabbed it —
it wasn't his fault.

"Here . . . I brought you this."
And he opened his hand:
a small silver compass
with a nice leather band.

"It could fit on your wrist
and show you the way."
And that's when Bart knew
there was nothing to say.

All of those rules
had taken their toll:
No running, no jumping,
no going for a stroll.

No joking, no smoking.
No crying, no lying,
and though they didn't say it,
of course . . . there's no flying.

"I'm sorry, I can't,"
Densy said, looking down,
a tear in his eye,
while he stared at the ground.

"All I wanted to do
was to fly out of here,
but now that it's blowing
and now that you're here. . . ."

"Just grab onto this corner,"
Bartholomew said.
"I was scared, too,
but I took off instead.

"And I'm *glad* that I did.
Oh, come on, just do it.
You know that you can.
In fact, you always knew it."

Densy reached out
and grasped at the sheet
but pulled away quickly,
a hasty retreat.

He backed up two steps
as Bartholomew rose.
The bedsheet ascended,
because when it goes,

it happens so fast —
in the blink of an eye —
and Densmore sat earthbound
just *watching* Bart fly.

"Wow — look at that.
You look really great."
And his voice started fading,
but Bart couldn't wait.

Pretty soon he was up
around five hundred feet.
And Densy just stood there
below, with his feet

planted firm on the ground,
which was next to some woods,
which was next to a school
where they had lots of *should*s

but even more *shouldn't*s,
with curfews and bells.
And if Densmore was sad,
well, Bart couldn't tell,

because pretty soon
he just turned to a dot,
but way, way down there
was one boy who might not

just follow the rules
for rules' sake anymore.
And as Bart drifted east
the school bell chimed . . .

He was lost in a cloud,
all white, bright, and endless.
In the midst of the mist,
he missed Densy. Now, friendless,

he floated and drifted
not uppish nor down,
just drifted and shifted
and listed around.

He glanced at the compass
but just didn't care,
for he now knew that "who"
mattered much more than "where."

"I hope he got back
to his dorm room okay.
I hope that there wasn't
too much heck to pay.

"I hope he remembers
to take out the boat.
I hope he keeps practicing
just how to float."

At that point, Bart noticed
the clouds racing by.
I must really be moving,
he thought. *Wow, wonder why. . . .*

And then the clouds gathered
and grew even darker.
He looked down below
to search for a marker,

but the land was all gone!
The storm blew and blew.
This wasn't just wind,
it was, well — something *new*.

"I've got to get down,"
Bart said with resolve.
The bedsheet was tearing;
it might soon dissolve.

Bartholomew tucked
his knees up to his chest.
He lowered his chin.
He hoped for the best.

The bedsheet was doing
two hundred or more.
It started to rip;
rain started to pour.

As a new gust of wind
sent him head over heels.
the bedsheet got tangled!
And that's how it feels

to drop from the sky
like a rock or a chair.
No, this wasn't *flying* . . .
this was falling through air!

It raged on like that
for an hour at least.
First it blew west
and then it blew east.

It carried him up;
it tumbled him down
like a carnival ride
going around and around.

But then after a while
the wind lost its rush.
The noise had died down.
The world was a hush.

Then soon it was gone,
not even a trace,
just a bright brilliant sun
to warm up his face.

Bartholomew glided
down ever so softly.
He clung to the corners.
He waved to an osprey.

His craft had become
just a large parachute,
without any wind
or direction to boot.

He clung to it tight
as he fluttered to earth.
I've never seen no *wind,*
he thought. *That's a first.*

But

down in the canyon
this sight was quite normal.
"Another one coming—
no need to be formal.

"Just ring the bell once
to announce our new guest,
and then let him settle.
It's usually best

"to give them a while
to get all adjusted,
to know what they're seeing
is a sight to be trusted,

"for our little village
can seem rather strange
when you're blown in from
desert, or mountain, or range."

As he drifted toward earth,
Bart swore he heard singing.
And then closer still,
he heard a bell ringing.

The parachute floated
down onto the sand.
The water was quiet,
and so was the land.

The air didn't move.
With no trace of a breeze,
the ocean was motionless,
just like the trees.

The cove was quite narrow
with thousand-foot cliffs
that soared toward the heavens.
Bartholomew sniffed

but couldn't smell *any*thing.
Nothing at all.
No breeze and no wind —
there was just a strange pall

that hung in the air,
and he just had to wonder
if winding up here
was the greatest of blunders.

The cove was so narrow,
the canyon so high —
with no wind down here
there was no way to fly!

I'm stuck here, he thought.
Might be here forever.
And forever's a long time,
a cousin of never.

He gathered the sheet
and trudged up the sand.
"Why, this was the stupidest
place I could land."

He pushed through a bramble,
climbed up a small rise,
looked over the top,
and to his surprise

saw the *strangest* collection
of things in the world
that cluttered the canyon
while five little girls

in olive-green uniforms
marched in a line,
singing a scout song
in perfect scout time.

Way off in the distance,
a large covered wagon
sat next to a flagpole
with all of its flags on:

Switzerland, Mexico,
Burma, and Spain.
Many were beautiful;
some were quite plain.

One from a country club,
one silhouette,
a set of cloth panels
that came from Tibet.

Bartholomew stood there
and surveyed the place.
There were traces of fliers
all over the place:

a piece of a blimp,
a tattered balloon,
the shell of an airplane.
He thought pretty soon

he might see the space shuttle
lying on its side.
He saw an umbrella —
"Now, that's quite a ride."

"Ha, ha! That's what I said!"
Bart heard from behind him.
"That's Nigel the Butler's —
he's stuffy; don't mind him.

"He's quite a good chap
when you get to know him.
He landed from London.
So, when did *you* blow in?"

Her name was Amelia
and she was a flier
or used to be one—
now she was "retired."

The hull of her plane
was a quaint little home:
a nice row of marigolds
with stepping-stones.

The right wing was missing
and so was the prop,
the other: a sundeck
with flight chair on top.

"Hey, don't I know you?"
Bartholomew said.
"Well, that'd be nice —
it would mean you're well read."

She stuck out her hand
and gave his a shake.
"Just call me 'Meelia.
My dog's name is Jake."

A dachshund was sniffing
the base of Bart's leg.
"He wants you to pet him.
C'mon, Jake — don't beg."

Bartholomew turned
and took in the canyon:
an odd set of structures,
but none looked abandoned.

A makeshift chalet,
an Indian lodge,
a weather balloon,
a '55 Dodge.

"Excuse me, where am I?"
Bartholomew said.
"Maybe I'm dreaming?
Or maybe I'm dead?"

"No, this is just *it*.
It's the end of the line.
It's where the wind takes you,
and frankly, it's fine.

"Just some getting used to
is all that's required.
There's lots of nice neighbors,
but rest now. You're tired."

"Wait — who *are* these neighbors?"
Bartholomew asked.
He was staring at one house
that looked like a raft.

"They all got blown in here
From someplace like you.
'Right place' and 'wrong time'
when the 'Big Windy' blew.

"That gal was a golfer
on number eighteen
when a nasty tornado
dropped in on her green,

"and that lady right there
with those big wooden shoes,
she was fixing her windmill
when she got the news.

"You can stay here with me
till we figure it out.
I'll get you some lunch
and dry clothes from the scouts."

"But why do you *stay* here?"
Bartholomew asked.
"Why not just climb out?
Fly away? Leave here *fast*?"

"Oh, that's not so easy,"
Amelia replied.
"The cliffs are straight up.
A couple have tried,

"but they only got up,
like, two hundred feet.
And with no wind down here,
what good is your sheet?"

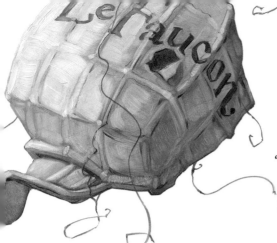

"Then why not build a boat
and just sail away?
Some wood and some oars
and a nice gentle day. . . ."

"The current's too strong,"
she said with a sigh.
"I know how you feel,
and, well, you can try,

"but it isn't much use.
There's no way to get out.
Even those surfers
have figured that out."

And there, sure enough,
a couple of dudes
just sat on the beach
looking rather subdued.

Bartholomew got it —
this place was like jail:
just ocean and cliffs —
and no way to make bail.

"Come on, now," she said.
"We'll go meet the others —
Pierre the balloonist
and the windsurfing brothers."

She motioned ahead
toward the center of "town."
And Bart said to himself,
What a place to come down.

Everyone welcomed
Bartholomew easily.
They passed their time well
(though you couldn't say "breezily").

'Meelia gave Bart
the back of her plane.
She loaned him a hammock —
he couldn't complain.

At night he would hear
a sweet flute from Nepal.
Some Sherpa got stuck
in a mountainous squall

and now lived next door
in the coolest of yurts.
He made them mint tea
and papaya desserts.

There were hikers and bikers,
a Swiss mountaineer,
three Sunday fishermen
blown from their pier,

a pioneer family
complete with their wagon,
a nice guy from China
whose kite was a dragon.

Bart made the rounds
each evening for tea,
an invite a night,
sometimes two or three.

A brand-new arrival
was quite the commodity.
Some wanted news;
some just loved the oddity.

The boy who could fly
with only a *sheet*!
Nigel said, "Splendid!"
The surfer said, "Sweeeeet."

But after a week
Bart got the old itch.
When he glanced at the sheet,
he started to twitch.

He gazed at the cliff
where an eagle was soaring,
turning in circles . . .
"Now, that's worth exploring.

"He looks like he's gliding
up there on a thermal,
which means there's some wind,
and if this infernal

"huge cliff wasn't here,
I could go get me some."
His mind began whirring;
it started to hummm.

"I bet these nice people
would give me a hand.
Maybe that's what they need:
some sort of a plan."

So Bart went and talked
to the Swiss mountaineer.
"*Nein!* Not on that cliff!
Those valls are too sheeeerrrr!"

"But you've still got your pick
and those things on your shoes. . . ."
The man shook his head,
and that wasn't good news.

He said it was hopeless
without some assistance.
"Just look at that cliff!
That's quite a distance!"

The next guy Bart tried
was the chap from Rangoon,
the one with the fifty-foot
weather balloon.

"Why don't we *try* it?"
Bart said, sounding brighter.
"*You* don't need the wind —
just air that is *lighter*."

The man pointed down
to a rip in the fabric,
a long twelve-foot tear.
It was sad, almost tragic.

"I've sewed and I've sewed,
but the thing always leaks.
I tried gluing once,
for almost three weeks.

"I'm afraid this balloon
is just useless old silk."
Right then he got teary
like he'd spilled his milk.

He looked like he needed
a hug from his mom.
And Bart shook his head.
"Why, this is just *wrong*. . . .

"They sit and they stare
at nothing at all.
They used to have guts —
why, that guy from Nepal

"climbed Everest twice!
How hard is a *canyon*?
I need some advice,
or at least a companion."

He sat with Amelia
on the edge of her wing.
She nodded her head —
she felt the same thing:

"We're stuck in the doldrums
down here. Bart, it's true.
Just try to make peace —
it's the best you can do."

But that made him sad,
and then sadder some more.
He was fine leaving home —
in fact, that's what home's for —

but it should be a *choice,*
not shoved down your throat.
Bart tossed an old bottle
to sea with a note.

But it washed back on shore
the very next day.
"She's right. This is home,
and now I'm here to stay."

Bart took to whittling
pieces of wood.
After a week,
he'd gotten quite good.

He carved several elephants,
funny giraffes,
four rocket ships,
some aardvarks for laughs.

Then one day when he
was out passing the time,
carving a turtle
the size of a dime,

he let out a yawn,
then looked up and squinted
'cause on the horizon,
a light flashed and glinted

and then disappeared.
It was gone just as fast.
"Oh, well," he said, shrugging.
"These things never last."

Hundreds of times
he'd imagined a ship
or a plane swooping in,
but they left in a blip.

He returned to the turtle
and finished the head,
then started the tail
but looked up instead

and right then he knew —
this wasn't some figment,
some wispy mirage. . . .
Why, this thing had *pigment*!

It seemed to be moving
at quite a nice clip,
soaring right toward him.
It wasn't a ship,

and it wasn't a plane. . . .
Why, if he had to guess,
Bart would say it was *Bart*
coming out of the west.

He could see the resemblance,
bedsheet and all.
Two arms were outstretched;
he was standing quite tall.

Why, that guy can fly,
Bart said to himself.
He's got nice technique,
if I say so myself.

And as he got closer
it all became clearer.
It wasn't a bedsheet,
for as it got nearer,

some writing appeared . . .
some sort of a *banner*.
The letters were fuzzy
and fancy and mannered,

but after a moment
they all became clear:
School Social on Saturday
Night — with Root Beer!

"Hmm, that's from a school —
I wonder who grabbed it.
(My school had one, too;
I wish I'd have nabbed it.)

"It looks pretty sturdy —
that guy is no fool.
In fact that guy is . . . is . . . IS . . .
DENSMORE HORATIO POOL!

"Oh, my goodness!" Bart said,
and he jumped with delight.
He watched Densy descend
and then bank to his right.

"That's him! That's Densmore!
Same jacket, same pants,
same crest on the pocket!"
Bart started to dance.

"Oh, *that's* it, good buddy!
You just keep on steering!"
Bart jumped up and down
as Densmore was nearing.

"Pull back on the corners!
That's good — now just beach her."
But Densmore was fine;
he had had a good teacher.

And over the weeks
he had really improved.
He rode with the wind
as it shifted and moved,

then Densmore touched down
with some seagulls in tow,
a soft three-point landing
with billow for show.

"Why, Densy, you made it!"
Bart said with a cackle.
"That's no easy flight
you decided to tackle."

"It's amazing!" said Densy,
"just like you said:
there wasn't much breeze —
it was pretty much dead —

"but when I took off
I got hit with a gust
and remembered you said,
'Don't fight it; just trust it.'

"And next thing I knew
I was up in the air
with the sun in my face
and the wind in my hair."

And then our friend Densy
just started to chuckle,
and Bart understood —
if you're one of the lucky

ones who gets to fly
even *once* in your life,
you're never the same,
but that comes with a price.

Because once you have flown
you just want it again,
but down in the valley
with no trace of wind,

a sheet was a sheet —
it just drooped to the ground.
"C'mon," Bart said softly.
"I'll show you around."

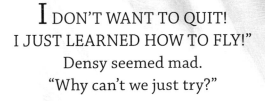

5

I DON'T WANT TO QUIT!
I JUST LEARNED HOW TO FLY!"
Densy seemed mad.
"Why can't we just try?"

Bart couldn't help smiling
at all of that passion —
he'd felt the same thing
right after *he'd* crashed in

this dead little cove
where the wind never blew.
They lay on their backs
and looked up at the moon.

"There's wind up on top,"
Bart said. "You can tell.
There are red-tailed hawks
and all of those gulls . . .

"they're catching the thermals.
I know 'cause I've seen it.
We just can't get *up* there . . .
We're stuck, and I mean it."

And that's when Bart told him
how no one would budge.
The climber quit climbing.
The scouts wouldn't trudge.

The sailors just sat
on the edge of the shore.
Even the golfer
had stopped shouting "fore."

"You sound just like they do,"
Dens said with contempt.
"It's one thing to fail,
but not to attempt it . . .

"All of those pep talks
for days in your tent!
I'm sorry," said Densy.
"I thought that you meant it."

The sharp tone took Bart
by a bit of surprise.
You can lose your own way
and not realize it

till someone you know grabs
your shoulders and shakes 'em.
Most people don't move
until someone else makes 'em.

"Well, maybe," Bart said,
"we can give it a go.
We'll ask them again —
they can only say no.

"With two of us now,
we don't need as much help —
a little equipment.
We'll do it ourselves."

Densmore agreed, and
they made out their list:
some rope from the Swiss guy
to climb through the mist.

"We'll need to stay dry,
and the sailors have ponchos.
We'll go ask the big one
'cause he's the main honcho.

"Amelia's goggles,
the scout master's mirror
(to signal the ground
once we've gotten nearer),

"a whole bunch of cookies
(the Girl Scouts have dozens).
We'll get us some shades
from those windsurfing cousins."

They weren't gonna stay
where the wind never blew.
And yeah, it was scary,
but they also knew

that once you decide,
it all gets much *clearer*.
And suddenly home
felt a little bit nearer.

The news traveled quickly,
as news tends to do
when you live in a place
where nothing is new.

The thought of a voyage
was special indeed,
so word of their trip
spread at light-e-ning speed.

"How *can* I assist you?"
Nigel inquired.
"I will say this gambit
is truly inspired.

"The vigor of youth
and some good derring-do,
a fine braided rope,
and a good sturdy shoe.

"Yes, it's quite a climb,
but if you've got the nerve,
and gumption, and guts,
and a good bit of verve,

you might just get out.
And though that's *our* loss. . . .
Please. Here — accept
my Victoria Cross."

Bart looked at the medal
attached to the ribbon
that shone in the sunlight,
and if he was given

to getting all mushy,
this sure would have done it.
"Yes, I'll wear it proudly,"
he said, and he hung it

around his own neck
while Densmore saluted.
Nigel did, too,
and even included

a click of the heels
and quick little nod,
and Bart realized
(though this sounds a bit odd)

that he wouldn't be flying now
for only just him.
This wasn't just fun,
and it wasn't a whim.

He'd be flying now for *all of them,*
children and scouts,
the ones who believed
and the ones who had doubts,

the Sherpa, the Swiss guy,
and all mountaineers,
all those who dreamed they could
conquer their fears

and hoist themselves up
on the end of a rope.
As the big day got closer,
the town gushed with hope.

The balloonist helped Densy
mend rips in his banner.
Amelia gave Bart
her own preflight planner:

a worn leather volume
for mapping the route,
with a nice little checklist
and pencil to boot.

The mountaineer
showed Bart his favorite technique
for securing a line
as you got near the peak.

The pioneers gave him
their own family Bible.
"We don't mean to scare you,
but we think that you're liable

"to need this up there
a lot more than we will.
Those cliffs look darn scary —
in fact, they look *evil*."

Bart promised he'd keep it
right next to his heart,
and then, pretty soon,
it was time to depart.

The Sherpa burned incense,
the scouts sang their songs,
and then before long
the whole town sang along.

Amelia moved forward
for final advice —
he didn't much need it,
but still it was nice.

"Keep your eyes open
and watch for those gusts.
The wind is your friend,
but you can't always trust it."

"Thanks," Bart replied
as he clung to the planner.
And then Nigel nodded
in Nigel-like manner.

The mountaineer tied
Bart and Densy together.
They yanked on the rope;
they glanced up at the weather:

a couple of clouds
at the top of the cliff
were moving along
at quite a nice clip.

"That looks pretty good,"
Bart said with a chuckle.
Densy agreed
and tightened his buckle,

and everyone clapped
as they moved toward the cliff.
"Aw, that doesn't look high . . .
we'll be there in a jiff."

Just don't look down,"
said Bart, "and I mean it."
(A drop's not a drop
till you're there and you've seen it,

a thousand feet up
while you cling to the rocks,
with both your legs shaking
right down to your socks.)

"I looked," Densy said.
"I just couldn't help it.
And then I got queasy,
and that's when I felt it

"come up in my throat.
And then I had this hunch
that, well — pretty soon —
I'd be losing my lunch."

"Come on," Bart said,
"just a little bit higher.
Why, this cliff is *nothing* —
you're Densmore the flier!

"You won't let a silly old rock
hold you back.
Just try to breathe deep —
and hold on to that sack."

They climbed a bit higher
and looked straight ahead.
Dens gripped his banner
just like Bart had said.

"My arms are so tired,"
Densmore complained.
"My legs can't hold on —
my back is in pain."

"Just a little bit farther,"
Bart shouted behind him.
"C'mon, Dens, don't quit."
But the words didn't find him —

all Densy could hear
was a high piercing whistle.
It wasn't a plane
and it wasn't a missile.

But still it was shrill,
and it screamed in his ear.
"Sorry," said Densy,
"I really can't hear!"

They yelled back and forth
and they tried to be heard,
and that's when Bart happened
to glance at a bird

who was hovering close
without flapping its wings,
held up by the *wind*
(which is one of things

that you think they'd have noticed
but neither one did).
As soon as they felt it,
they 'bout flipped their lid.

"*That's wind!*" Bart yelled.
"Do you feel that, Densy?"
A thrill in his voice —
you might call it frenzy.

They pulled and they scrambled
and climbed up the cliff,
hand over hand,
pausing once for a whiff

of the salt air, now blowing —
the scent of the sea.
They breathed it in deep —
it felt wild and free.

"C'mon, now, I see it.
We're right near the top!"
And there, sure enough,
at the top of the rocks

a meadow stretched out,
a broad field of green,
poppies and mustard,
a heavenly scene.

The gulls were all calling him,
cawing like laughter.
They cackled as if
they knew what he was after.

"My gosh," Densy said
as he got to the crest.
"It's beautiful, Bart.
You think we can rest?"

"Sure, catch your breath.
This is it, pal. We made it.
That comes with a price,
and trust me, we paid it."

Densmore breathed deep —
it had been quite a climb.
But much more than that
they had had quite a time.

And neither one said
what the other one knew:
that this was good-bye,
and as soon as they flew

off that cliff, side by side,
it might be the last day
that they flew in formation.
"C'mon, Dens — this way."

They walked to the edge
and looked at the sea,
Dens with his banner
and Bart with his sheet.

"Wait till they see me
swoop into that school!
I'll buzz that whole courtyard!
That sounds pretty cool."

But then they got quiet
for obvious reasons.
Summer was over. . . .
these things ran in seasons.

Soon Bart would be doing
his spelling and math,
science reports
complete with a graph.

Up until now
it had felt pretty awful —
not much fun at school
(well — not much that was lawful).

But since he'd been gone,
some *questions* had grown,
and all of the answers,
it seemed, were at home.

Did ancient Rome fall
or did someone push it?
Was space always quiet
or did someone shush it?

Could fish really fly?
And what about squirrels?
What about Mars?
And what about girls?

What about gravity?
Where did it come from?
When did time start?
That's quite a conundrum.

And going back to school
seemed a little bit better
'cause all of those problems
and numbers and letters

might be a nice change
from just chasing the wind —
some yin for his yang.
It was time to begin.

They stood at the edge,
looked out at the sea,
held on to their sails . . .
and counted to three.

Down in the valley
they peered toward the sky,
looking for boys
who said they could fly.

"I shoulda gone up there.
I shoulda — it's true."
Amelia kept pacing
(her dachshund did, too).

Nigel the butler
kept winding his watch.
The golfer just sat there
and guzzled her scotch.

The fishermen squinted
and scanned the horizon.
Everyone down there
had focused their eyes on

the sky right above them
where birds were still gliding.
"C'mon, boys — where are you?
Come out now. Quit hiding."

And just when a couple
had given up hope
and Amelia was right at
the end of her rope,

a scout pointed up
(as scouts tend to do).
"Right there! Ten o'clock!"
And then out of the blue

two gliders emerged,
soaring and swooping.
The town started clapping
and yelling and whooping.

"Oh, look at them go!
Gosh, look at that sight!"
Amelia got misty
watching their flight,

for she thought that she might
never see it again,
and she couldn't help thinking
these boys were now men.

They leveled off smoothly
at five thousand feet,
the sun up above them,
the clouds at their feet.

Bart glanced at his compass
which pointed due east.
They could fly side by side
for a while at least.

Then Densy would peel off,
heading due north,
and Bart would head south.
He'd plotted a course

as best he remembered,
and though it was fuzzy,
he never felt lost.
And he wasn't — or was he?

No, you're not really lost
when it's making you smile,
so they stretched out their wings
and just flew for a while.

They soared on in silence
as guests of the wind.
There was nothing to say.
They were almost like twins.

Then after a bit,
he heard Densy exclaim,
"Right there, Bart — I see it!"
And there was some rain

that was nasty and gray
as it clung to the coast,
a dark little town
that was nothing to boast

about. Still, it was home,
and Densy was grinning.
And Bart knew each end
was just a beginning.

His friend was already
leaning for home.
"Go ahead," Bart said.
"Can you make it alone?"

"Oh, yeah," Dens replied —
he was already going.
"I'll see you next summer."
And Bart nodded, knowing

he probably wouldn't,
but that was okay
'cause he knew he and Densy
were best friends to stay.

Bart flew for hours
on a south-southeast heading.
He flew pretty fast,
and weather permitting,

he might make it home
with some daylight to spare.
He hung out with some geese —
it was pleasant up there.

Then after a while,
he started to tire.
Of course, Bart was good
(the best bedsheet flier),

but *no* sheet is made
for this kind of distance.
Your arms will get tired
despite your persistence,

and so it was lucky
that after nine hours,
with one nasty headwind
and two gentle showers,

Bart spotted a light
off on the horizon
and then saw some more,
then all sorts of lights on.

The buildings, the houses,
the streetlights and cars,
the lights in the windows,
the lights in the bars,

the theaters, the shops,
his neighborhood, too —
Bart tipped the sheet
and sped up as he flew

toward the center of town,
then turned at the light,
descended a little,
then made a sharp right

at a street that he knew
like the back of his hand,
from tag and touch football,
his lemonade stand.

Bartholomew slowed
as a good flier should.
He billowed the sail —
he'd gotten quite good —

and gently touched down
on the edge of his lawn.
"It's nice to be back. . . .
Long time to be gone."

And sure, we could tell you
what happened that night,
but you can imagine,
and, well . . . you'd be right.

His mother fell over.
She hugged him and kissed him.
She wanted to kill him
'cause, gosh, she had missed him.

His dad even got
a big tear in his eye,
and that was the first time
Bart saw his dad cry.

"You're grounded, young man!
No more bedsheets for you.
I'm nailing that window —
that's it, boy. You're through."

But it's just 'cause they loved him
and they were so worried.
(These kids seem to grow up
in such a big *hurry*!)

But then, when Bart told them
the things he had seen —
the mountains, those pirates,
these things from a dream,

Amelia, the Sherpa,
the weather balloon,
the Swiss guy, the surfers,
the man from Rangoon,

Densmore, his school,
and how Bart had taught him
to fly away quick
before they had caught him,

the way that the air
makes you float, soar, and dive,
and much more than that,
makes you feel alive . . .

his folks got another
big tear in their eye.
But this one was sweet,
and not salty, and why?

'Cause deep down inside them,
both of them knew
that the best thing a mom
or a dad ought to do

was to let kids take off
and let go of their hand,
and just watch them fly . . .
'cause they already can.

Back in his room
Bart looked toward his window
all cozy and warm,
but the places he'd been to

kept spinning and dancing
inside of his head.
And that's when it hit him:
a boat for a bed!

Or a big floating surfboard
with lots of balloons . . .
the pirates would love that —
"They'd throw me doubloons."

Or how 'bout a car
that can drive underwater —
make friends with a sea horse
and race with the otters?

And that's when Bartholomew
let out a yawn
and fluttered his eyes,
and soon he was gone

to see all the things
that were left to be seen
from in here to out there
and each place in between.

THE END